D1264091

GHOST DETECTORS

Yo Ho No!

BOOK 13

BY
DOTTI ENDERLE

ILLUSTRATED BY
HOWARD MCWILLIAM

magic
wagon

visit us at www.abdopublishing.com

Published by Magic Wagon, a division of the ABDO Group, PO Box
398166, Edina, MN 55439. Copyright © 2014 by Abdo Consulting
Group, Inc. International copyrights reserved in all countries. All
rights reserved. No part of this book may be reproduced in any
form without written permission from the publisher.

Calico Chapter Books™ is a trademark and logo of Magic Wagon.

Printed in the United States of America, North Mankato, MN.
102013
012014

 This book contains at least 10% recycled materials.

Text by Dotti Enderle
Illustrations by Howard McWilliam
Edited by Stephanie Hedlund and Rochelle Baltzer
Cover and interior design by Jaime Martens

Library of Congress Cataloging-in-Publication Data

Enderle, Dotti, 1954- author.
  Yo ho no! / by Dotti Enderle ; illustrated by Howard McWilliam.
      pages cm. -- (Ghost detectors ; book 13)
  Summary: When Malcolm and Dandy set out to get a picture of
a ghostly pirate ship, they find themselves reeled in by the pirates-
-and they have to agree to dig up the captain's buried treasure or
they will never be allowed to leave.
  ISBN 978-1-62402-001-8
1. Ghost stories. 2. Pirates--Juvenile fiction. 3. Treasure troves-
-Juvenile fiction. 4. Best friends--Juvenile fiction. 5. Humorous
stories. [1. Ghosts--Fiction. 2. Pirates--Fiction. 3. Buried treasure-
-Fiction. 4. Best friends--Fiction. 5. Friendship--Fiction. 6.
Humorous stories.] I. McWilliam, Howard, 1977- illustrator. II.
Title. III. Series: Enderle, Dotti, 1954- Ghost Detectors ; bk. 13.
  PZ7.E69645Yo 2014
  813.6--dc23   2013025335

Contents

The *Flying* Hornswaggle

Malcolm sat up, stretched, and yawned. Yes! Saturday! The laziest day of the week.

He went to the kitchen and poured a bowl of Toasty-Os cereal. Then, he grabbed a spoon and rushed into the living room to watch his favorite TV program, *Ghost Stalkers*. He'd never missed a single episode.

The hosts of the show were Bob, Nick, and Carol—three ghost hunters who travel

from city to city, searching for phantoms, apparitions, and spirit activity.

"Welcome to this week's episode," Nick said, holding a satellite thingie over his head.

Malcolm never understood why they used such clumsy equipment. Their meters and sensors were about the size of his TV. More than once, a ghost had picked one up and bopped Nick over the head with it. Malcolm had done a lot of ghost hunting, and one thing's for sure . . . you never let a ghost touch your tools!

He'd e-mailed the hosts four times to suggest they get an Ecto-Hand-Held-Automatic-Heat-Sensitive-Laser-Enhanced Specter Detector. When it comes to ghost detecting, it was the best.

Malcolm had just bitten into a spoonful of cereal when Bob said, "Today, we're

stalking the bay area. There've been quite a few sightings lately of the legendary ghost ship, the *Flying Hornswaggle*." The camera panned across the beach.

Malcolm nearly choked on a Toasty-O. Whoa! He couldn't believe it. This wasn't just any bay area. It was the one just across the bridge! The Ghost Stalkers had filmed here? If only he'd known!

"As you know," Bob continued, "the *Flying Hornswaggle* was commanded by Captain Crusty Scab, the nastiest pirate to ever set sail."

"Yes," Carol added, "he was famous for raiding, plundering, and robbing passing ships. And after taking all the loot, he'd run his victim's underwear up the ship's mast."

Even though cereal milk dribbled down his chin, Malcolm kept his eyes glued to

the TV. The camera flashed to Nick again. He was standing by a blond woman with a huge gap in her front teeth. "It was ssso ssscary!" she whistled. "I was sssitting alone, watching the wavesss when I heard a ssship's horn."

"A ship's horn?" Nick asked.

"Yesss. It sssounded like thisss: *Bell-oo-ga*!"

Nick nodded. It was a pretty impressive imitation.

"Ssso I looked up and there it wasss." She turned and pointed toward the gray clouds. "The *Hornssswaggle*, sssailing across the sssky."

"It must have been terrifying," Nick said.

The woman clutched her hands to her chest. "I was ssscared sssilly."

"Can you describe it?" he asked her.

Her eyes grew wide. "Its sssails billowed. Lightning sssparked all around it. And instead of a flag, it flew a huge pair of men'sss long johnsss."

"That would definitely be the *Hornswaggle*," Nick agreed.

Wow! Malcolm had no idea the famous *Flying Hornswaggle* had been spotted so close to where he lived. This was fantastic!

The Ghost Stalkers interviewed a few more people who all gave the same

description. Then, the three of them spent the night on the beach, aiming their doodads toward the sky. They waited and watched. But no matter how high they turned up their gadgets' controls, the *Flying Hornswaggle* never appeared.

Malcolm flipped off the TV. The *Flying Hornswaggle*! So close! He paced the floor, his mind racing. The Ghost Stalkers couldn't spot the *Flying Hornswaggle* . . . "But I can," Malcolm said out loud.

His ghost detector could detect anything from the teeniest ghostly flea to a massive flying ship. He'd find the *Hornswaggle*, get plenty of pictures, and send them to Bob, Carol, and Nick. 'Cause seriously, they were using all the wrong gizmos.

Malcolm planned it all out. Tomorrow he and his best friend and fellow ghost hunter, Dandy, would spend the day at the beach.

Smooth Sailing

Malcolm led Dandy down to his basement lab.

"You're being awfully quiet," Dandy said, following Malcolm one slow step at a time. "I don't like it when you're quiet."

This was a delicate matter. Malcolm had to approach it with caution.

"Why'd you call?" Dandy asked. "You made it sound like it was life or death."

"It's more like fame and fortune," Malcolm told him.

Dandy perked up. "Fame and fortune? I'm in."

Malcolm hoped so! He powered up his ghost detector. *Bleep-bleep.* He let his ghostly dog, Spooky, come out to play.

Yip! Yip! Spooky bounded and wagged his tail at Dandy.

Malcolm knew there was no way to break the news gently. So he drew a deep breath and said it at Band-Aid ripping speed. "We're going to the beach."

Dandy froze. His face turned a sickly shade of green. He gulped, turned, and almost made it to the stairs before Malcolm grabbed him by his T-shirt and jerked him back. He kept a tight grip on him so he couldn't get away.

Spooky thought it was all a game. He did figure eights between Malcolm and Dandy's feet. *Yip! Yip!*

"Don't you want fame and fortune?" Malcolm asked.

Dandy slumped. "Not if it means going to the beach. I'm allergic to the beach."

Here we go again. "Dandy, you're not allergic to the beach. Nobody is allergic to the beach."

"I am! Every time we go I end up with blisters on my toes. Even at night when the sand's cold and clammy, they swell up like hot dog weenies."

"Then wear flip-flops," Malcolm suggested.

"I've tried. I still get blisters on my toes. And flip-flops make a popping noise

12

when I walk. I can't sneak up on anyone. What if I want to sneak up on someone?"

Hmmm, Malcolm thought. *He does have a point. Getting pictures of the* Flying Hornswaggle *might take some sneaking.* "Why don't you wear beach shoes then?"

Dandy lifted his foot, kicking it right through Spooky. "Do you know how painful it is to get sand in your shoe? Every time I take a step it feels like my foot is being sawed in half. I'd rather have blisters on my toes."

"It's all in your mind, Dandy. Besides, once we have fame and fortune, you can buy the best blister cream on the market."

Dandy plopped down on the beanbag chair. Spooky pounced onto his lap and fell through. Dandy leaned forward, covering his face with his hands. "Why does it have to be the beach?"

Malcolm had to convince him. He couldn't do this all alone. "Because we're going to take a picture of the *Flying Hornswaggle.*"

Dandy peeped through his fingers. "The flying what?"

"The *Flying Hornswaggle.* It's a famous ghost ship. It was even featured on *Ghost Stalkers.* Lots of people have seen it, but

no one's ever taken a picture of it . . . until now." Malcolm waggled his eyebrows and grinned.

But Dandy wasn't through grumbling. "Why a ship?" he whined. "Why not a haunted rowboat at the lake? Or a haunted raft on the river? Or even better, a haunted water noodle in the pool?"

Malcolm rolled his eyes. "That's small time. This is the *Flying Hornswaggle*. It's been spotted off the coasts of India, South Africa, and Greenland. There have been tales told about it for centuries. This is our big chance! If we get just one picture of it, we'll be rich. And the Ghost Stalkers will interview us!"

"Are you sure we'll be famous?" Dandy asked.

Malcolm couldn't hold in his excitement. "Yes. Our picture of the

Hornswaggle will be printed in all the popular magazines. *Time. Newsweek. National Geographic.*"

"And *The Bigfoot Journal*?" Dandy asked.

"Are you kidding? It'll be on the front page of that one," Malcolm assured him. "I bet we'll get a free subscription for life."

Dandy grinned. "That's pretty awesome." His mouth twitched as he thought it over. "When would we go?"

"Tomorrow," Malcolm answered. "My dad is going to drop us off."

Dandy smiled. "If it means we'll be rich and famous, I guess I can brave it."

"Just think," Malcolm said to Dandy, "we can have anything we want once we snap that picture of the *Flying Hornswaggle*. We'll go on tour, traveling from city to city. From country to country! We'll meet

kings and emperors and presidents. And we'll autograph a gazillion copies of our *Flying Hornswaggle* photo for all of our adoring fans."

"Do you really think we'll see it?" Dandy asked.

"The *Flying Hornswaggle* is unpredictable. We'll have to be in the right place at the right time. But that shouldn't be a problem."

He didn't want to tell Dandy that the only way to ensure getting that picture was to stay out on the beach all day.

"Okay," Dandy said. "I'll pack lots of blister cream."

"And don't worry," Malcolm assured him, "once we get that picture, just like the *Hornswaggle*, things will be smooth sailing."

A Day at the Beach

Malcolm put on his swim trunks and grabbed his backpack of ghost gear. "Let's go, Dandy. My dad's waiting."

"Ready." Dandy clomped forward in a pair of purple rain boots, an orange plastic poncho, rubber gloves, and a football helmet.

Malcolm rolled his eyes. "Wow! I'm afraid you might scare away the ghosts."

Dandy stumbled toward him. "I'm not taking any chances."

Malcolm slumped. "Dandy, there is no such thing as a beach allergy."

"That's easy for you to say," Dandy argued. "You don't get blisters on your toes."

Malcolm sighed. "Fine."

When they got into the car, his dad asked Dandy, "Are you going wade fishing?"

"No, sir," Dandy answered. "I'm allergic to the beach."

Malcolm's dad's eyebrows raised like two question marks. He looked at Malcolm. "Allergic to the beach?"

Malcolm shook his head. "Don't ask."

As they rambled to the bay, Malcolm's dad laid down some rules. "Use plenty of sunscreen. Don't swim out too far. And watch out for jellyfish."

"Jellyfish!" Dandy's voice echoed through his helmet.

Malcolm nudged him and whispered, "Don't worry. We're not even going in the water."

"Oh yeah," he whispered back.

As soon as they crossed the bridge, Malcolm took a huge whiff of that wonderful ocean air—salty, crisp, and a little sticky.

"Here you go," his dad said, pulling up. "I'll be back around five."

Malcolm grabbed his backpack and hopped out. "Let's go."

Dandy didn't move an inch. His eyes filled with horror. He looked down at the beach like it was shark-infested waters. "It's like poison ivy."

Malcolm gruffed. "You're being silly."

"If one grain touches my toe, I'll have clown feet."

Malcolm's dad turned back. "Are you getting out or not?"

"Here, hold this," Malcolm said, handing Dandy his backpack. He squatted down. "Hop on."

Dandy jumped onto Malcolm's back, nearly knocking him to the ground. Malcolm heaved him up higher.

"Are you sure you'll be okay?" his dad asked.

Malcolm nodded. "We'll be fine." As long as he didn't collapse from carrying Dandy around.

They said good-bye. Then Malcolm trudged across the sand, carrying Dandy piggyback. *Ooof!* Dandy's orange poncho was stickier than the ocean air.

They finally reached the pier and Malcolm dropped Dandy on it with an

Umph! Then he checked out the crowd.

Dandy took off his helmet and gloves. "Won't all these people take pictures of the *Hornswaggle,* too?"

Malcolm looked around. "I don't

think so." Luckily, the sun was shining brighter than a UFO. "See? They're all sitting under giant umbrellas that block their view. They'll never see a thing."

Unfortunately, the umbrellas blocked Malcolm's view, too. He had to find a spot out in the open. "Let's go over here." They settled close to a guy wearing a straw hat.

"This is perfect," he told Dandy.

"Not really," the guy in the hat said. "I've been here for two hours. Not a single bite."

"Oh, we're not here to fish," Malcolm said. "Just to take pictures." He nodded toward the camera hanging around his neck.

The man nodded and went back to fishing. Malcolm got busy, setting up for the picture of a lifetime. He opened his

pack and powered up his ghost detector. *Bleep-bleep-bleep.* Without taking it out, he pointed it up.

"What's that noise?" Straw Hat Man asked, looking at Malcolm's pack.

Malcolm thought fast. "Uh . . . it's a sonar . . . to attract fish."

"Let's hope it works," the man said. "I don't want to go home empty-handed."

Neither do I, Malcolm thought. He checked the skies. Yep, the ghost detector was working just fine. A parasailing ghost flew by. "Wheeee!" she yelled as she sailed past.

Malcolm and Dandy sat and looked upward.

"How long do you think we'll have to wait?" Dandy asked.

Malcolm shrugged. "Probably not long."

They kept their gaze on the sky. Five minutes . . . ten minutes . . . fifteen minutes.

Mr. Straw Hat glanced over at Malcolm. "Your sonar doesn't work."

Malcolm was beginning to think the same thing. Where is the *Hornswaggle*?

The man stood and handed his fishing rod to Dandy. "I'm going to grab a soda. Would you hold on to this for me while I'm gone?"

Dandy looked like the guy had handed him a snake. "Oh . . . uh . . . I'm not very good at fishing."

"Don't worry. You won't catch anything." The man stood and strolled away.

Dandy sat down and dangled his feet from the pier. "Be sure and tell me when the *Hornswaggle* shows up."

"Aye-aye," Malcolm joked.

A few moments later—*"Ahhhh!"*—something snatched Dandy's hook and rocketed through the water like it was attached to a speedboat. The fishing reel hummed as the string unwound from the spool.

"Malcolm! Malcolm! I've caught something!"

"Reel it in!" Malcolm shouted.

Dandy tried. The rod was bowed like a tree limb and the knob spun out of control. "I can't! It's a big one!"

Malcolm couldn't believe what he was seeing. "Must be a barracuda."

Dandy tugged and tugged and tugged, then snap! The fishing string hit the end of the spool. But that didn't stop the superfish. It kept racing away, taking Dandy with it! "No!"

Malcolm reached out just in time and grabbed Dandy by his poncho. But the fish was too strong. Had Dandy hooked a whale? Malcolm dug his heels in, trying not to slide to the edge. He held Dandy. Dandy held the rod. And they pulled hard, playing a vicious game of tug-o-war with the fish.

They heaved and yanked and tugged. Then Malcolm happened to look up. A dark cloud swirled in the distance. Lightning flickered. Just above the horizon, the *Flying Hornswaggle* sailed in full glory. Its gray hull bobbed along. Its sails puffed in the wind. And raised high

on the mast was a flapping pair of long
john underwear.

"No! Not now." Malcolm couldn't reach
his camera—not without letting Dandy be
dragged away by a monstrous mackerel.

"Let go of the rod!" he yelled to Dandy.

"What?"

"Let go of the rod!"

Dandy fiercely shook his head. "I can't do that. The man in the straw hat would be awfully mad."

"It's okay," Malcolm assured him. "When we're rich and famous, we'll buy him a new one."

Dandy hung on.

"Let go!" Malcolm bellowed.

Snap! Just then, the fishing line broke, sending Malcolm and Dandy spilling backward onto the pier.

Malcolm jumped up and grabbed his camera, but it was too late. The *Flying Hornswaggle* had disappeared.

Kidnapped!

"It'll be back," Malcolm said. "I know it will." He reached into his pack and pulled out some juice boxes. He handed one to Dandy.

"Are we going to sit here all day?" Dandy asked.

Malcolm nodded. "If that's what it takes."

They were still watching the skies an hour later when rain clouds began to roll in. Dandy put his helmet back on.

People quickly folded their umbrellas and left the pier.

The wind grew stronger, flapping and whipping Dandy's poncho. "Malcolm?"

"Hang on," Malcolm said. He adjusted his ghost detector.

"Malcolm?" Dandy said again.

"Watch the sky, Dandy. With this eerie weather, I'm sure the *Hornswaggle* will appear at any moment."

"Malcolm, I can't see a thing."

Malcolm turned around. Dandy's poncho had blown up over his helmet and twisted around his neck. He looked like a big orange Tootsie Pop.

"Hold still." Malcolm tugged Dandy free from his plastic wrapper.

Dandy tucked the bottom of the poncho into his shorts. "Thanks. It felt like I was trapped in a beach ball."

Then they heard it. *Bell-oo-ga!* The mighty horn of the *Flying Hornswaggle.*

Malcolm pointed. "Look!"

An enormous black cloud floated toward them. Lightning zigged and zagged as the ghostly ship sailed out.

"Wow!" Dandy shouted. "It's as big as a regular ship!"

Malcolm lifted his camera. "Bigger." He focused the lens and snapped picture after picture after picture.

The ship cruised closer.

"This is fantastic!" Malcolm cheered.

Dandy tugged on Malcolm's sleeve. "Uh . . . Malcolm . . . the *Hornswaggle* is

getting awfully close. What if it decides to drop an anchor and conk us in the head?"

"Don't worry," Malcolm told him. "The *Hornswaggle* never comes into port. It's doomed to sail forever." As soon as he said it, the ship turned and headed back toward the cloud.

Malcolm couldn't believe it! He was one of the few people in history who'd actually seen the *Flying Hornswaggle*. "Wait till the Ghost Stalkers see these pictures!"

"Yeah," Dandy said. "They might put us on their show."

"Are you kidding? They'll make us regulars!"

Malcolm reached down to turn off his ghost detector. Suddenly—*whap!*—a huge net fell from the sky.

"What's going—" Malcolm never finished the sentence. The net swooped, trapping them like a school of tuna.

"Malcolm," Dandy squeaked, "what's happening?"

Malcolm gulped. "Hang on tight, Dandy! We're being kidnapped by the *Hornswaggle*'s crew!"

Captain Crusty Scab

The net lifted higher and higher. And if things couldn't get any worse, it started to pour.

Malcolm wiggled to his bag, trying to shut off the ghost detector. No use.

The ship grew closer and closer. Ew! The bottom was covered in icky moss, snails, and barnacles.

"This is crazy," he said to Dandy.

But Dandy had been caught upside down. Rain was filling his helmet.

"Blurdle-durdle," Dandy gurgled.

"Hang on, Dandy," Malcolm said. "Try not to drown."

Dandy made an A-OK sign with his fingers. "Blurgle-flurgle."

Finally, they were close enough to hear the pirate crew. "Heave! Heave!"

Dandy struggled. "Hurgle-murgle."

"Bring 'em in," one of the pirates called.

Then, with a hearty pull, the net swung over and—*oomph!*—the boys were plopped onto the poop deck.

"Are you okay?" Malcolm asked Dandy.

Dandy managed to wiggle himself upright. Water poured from his helmet. "I am now that I can breathe."

At least up here it stopped raining. Malcolm wondered how high they were.

The crew of ghastly ghost pirates leered over them, holding pistols, daggers, and rope. Malcolm had never seen such an ugly bunch of scalawags in his life. They could win first prize at a Halloween carnival.

Malcolm's heart thumped. "Dandy, next time remind me to pack my ghost zapper."

"If there is a next time," Dandy said through chattering teeth.

One of the pirates knelt down in front of them. The bandana tied on his head covered his left eye. His other eye sort of boggled around.

"Is he looking at us?" Dandy whispered.

Malcolm half-shrugged within the binding ropes. "Hard to say."

But what really scared the bejeepers out of Malcolm was the dagger that the boggle-eyed pirate held clenched in his teeth.

"Listen," Malcolm said, trying not to upset old Boggle-Eye, "we have to be back by five or my dad will have a fit."

Boggle-Eye removed the dagger. "A fit, huh?"

Malcolm half-nodded.

"Well," Boggle-Eye said, "imagine the worst fit your pappy can throw."

Malcolm remembered his dad pitching a fit when Grandma Eunice accidentally put her red bowling shirt in the wash with all the white clothes. Dad looked pretty silly going to work all week wearing pink shirts.

Boggle-Eye got closer, his breath as foul as asparagus. "Believe me. Pirates can throw a fit so big, it'll shake the dandruff from your hair."

Dandy dug his nails into Malcolm's arm and said, "We sure don't want to see that, Mr. Pirate. We'll be real cooperative."

Boggle-Eye stood and moved back into the circle of ghosts.

Malcolm had never felt so trapped in his life. Not even the time a ghost had hung him by his undies on a moose antler. "S-s-so what are you going to do with us?"

A filthy pirate with a nasty scar across his cheek grinned. "What'd ya say, men? Shall we string them up on the mast and let the gulls peck out their eyes?"

"No, no, no!" Dandy begged. "No eye pecking!"

Boggle-Eye patted the left side of his bandana. "It don't hurt . . . much."

A skinny pirate in a floppy hat stepped up. "Maybe we should shoot them from the cannon and see how far they fly."

Malcolm half-shook his head. "I don't think Dandy and I are qualified to perform

as human cannonballs."

"But I do have my helmet," Dandy pointed out.

Malcolm glared at him. "You're not helping."

"You know what I think?" the scarred pirate said. "I think we should let *him* decide."

The circle of ghosts parted. Standing tall was a giant of a man. His gray striped pants were tucked into tall black boots. A filthy blue coat covered his shredded white shirt. His beard formed a wonky *W* on his chin. And a scrawny parrot sat perched on his tricorn hat.

This was indeed the nastiest pirate ever to set sail—Captain Crusty Scab.

Land Ho, Mateys!

Malcolm froze. How had he gotten them into such a mess?

The captain grinned down at the boys, flashing a mouthful of rotted teeth, all clumped with seaweed. "Arrrrr, looks like we've caught a couple of live ones."

"That's right," Malcolm said. "Alive. We don't belong on a ghost ship."

Dandy nodded. "So if you'll just lower us back down, we'll pretend this whole

thing never happened."

"Quiet, you loony landlubbers!"

"Landlubbers!   Landlubbers!" the parrot echoed.

Crusty looked up at the bird, eyes crossed. "So what do you think, Squat?"

"You named your parrot Squat?" Malcolm said. "Don't most parrots have names like Polly or Pete or Crackers?"

"I said quiet!" Crusty barked. Then he heaved a large sigh. "Okay, since you asked." The captain whistled and Squat fluttered down from his hat to his shoulders. "Take a look at his legs."

Malcolm did. "Wow! He doesn't have any."

It was true. Squat's claws looked like they were glued to his belly.

"So, Squat," Captain Scab continued, "do we keep them or throw them overboard?"

"Overboard! Overboard!" Squat demanded.

"Wait!" Dandy cried. "We're miles and miles above the ocean. I don't think we'd survive the fall."

Crusty leaned down and glared. "Do you think I care?"

"Nope. Nope," Squat squawked.

The captain stroked his W beard. "Or better yet . . ." He seized the hilt of his sword and whipped it from his sash.

Dandy gripped Malcolm hard. "Oh no, he's going to run us through!"

But when Crusty pulled out his sword, the blade sliced through the sash that held up his striped pants. They dropped to his boots, revealing some scratchy red underwear. No wonder he was grumpy.

"Arrrr, I hate when that happens." He pulled his pants up and tied a knot at the waist to hold them in place. Then Captain Scab held up his sword, ready to plunge it straight through them.

Dandy dug his fingernails into Malcolm's arm. "We're doomed. We're doomed."

Squat fluttered his wings. "Doomed. Doomed."

Malcolm clamped his eyes shut and half-buried them in his hands. He couldn't stand the sight of blood. Especially his own.

But instead of running them through—*snip! snip! snip!*—Crusty used the sword to cut open the net.

"You know, Captain," Boggle-Eye said to him, "we could've just opened it up for you. Now you've ruined a perfectly good net."

"Nobody asked you," Crusty yelled, bopping Boggle-Eye on the head. "But since you're such a smarty-pants, you can be the one to mend it."

Boggle-Eye rolled his eye and sighed.

Crusty curled his lip, revealing a particularly nasty strand of seaweed. "I'll take this." He snatched up Malcolm's pack.

"What? No!" Malcolm exclaimed. There went his ghost detector! What if the captain turned it off? Would the ship disappear? Would he and Dandy fall like asteroids from the sky?

Crusty pointed a scabby finger at them. "Clap 'em in irons!"

Dandy's eyes doubled in size. "Uh-oh. I don't like the sound of that."

Boggle-Eye and Scar-Cheek came forward with heavy shackles. They clamped them around Malcolm and Dandy's wrists.

"Let's go," Scar-Cheek said to them.

Captain Scab held up his hand. "Wait!"

Everyone froze.

"Take the little one's armor."

Boggle-Eye grabbed Dandy's helmet. Scar-Cheek grabbed his rain boots. And the other ghosts bellowed with laughter as the two pirates pulled and yanked, stretching Dandy like he was a rubber band.

"Malcolm! Help!"

But what could Malcolm do?

Finally, Dandy popped out of his armor.

"Good," Crusty said. "Now take them below."

The long chains of their shackles jingled and jangled as they were led down to a cell below the deck.

"You won't be escaping this," Scar-Cheek said, rattling the door to show that it was locked tight.

Malcolm gripped the bars. "What's the captain going to do with us?"

"I'm sure he's got special plans for you."

With that, the pirates sneered and stalked off.

"What do we do now?" Dandy asked.

Malcolm looked down. They were standing ankle deep in stinky, gray water. "We won't be sitting down."

Dandy drooped. "I wish they hadn't taken my rain boots. This water is freezing."

"Yeah," Malcolm agreed, his arms prickling from the cold. "That's too bad."

The ship rocked and creaked like a seesaw. Malcolm grabbed the bars to keep from swaying.

Dandy grabbed the bars, too. He turned a sickly, puke-tastic shade of green. "You better stand back. That pancake I ate for breakfast is flipping again."

Malcolm examined their surroundings. "We've got to find a way out."

"Out of the handcuffs, the cell, or the ship?" Dandy asked.

"All of the above. Seriously, if we're not back by five, my dad's going to ground me for weeks."

The boat continued to teeter-totter, and Malcolm continued to worry. Especially about what might be swimming around in that shallow water sloshing at his feet. Just as he was about to give up hope, the cargo hatch opened.

Captain Scab clomped down the rickety steps. Squat squatted on his shoulder. "How do you lads like your new home?"

Dandy poked out his lower lip like he might cry. "We have to live here?"

The captain crossed his arms and leaned against the cell. "Unless you blokes want to handle a special task for me."

"Blokes. Blokes. Blokes." Squat taunted.

Malcolm gulped. "A task? You mean like swab the deck or bail water or man the crow's nest?"

Crusty waved it off. "None of that silliness. Any old sailor can do those chores."

Squat whistled. "Ahoy, sailor!"

"What I have in mind," the captain continued, "takes a certain skill."

Malcolm's fear turned to curiosity. "What type of skill?"

The captain pulled a piece of rolled paper from the new sash on his trousers. "Can you read a map?"

Squat turned his head left and right. "Which way? Which way?"

"Are you kidding?" Malcolm said, standing tall and proud. "Of course I can." Though he never needed to. His dad had a GPS system in the car, and a robotic lady always gave them directions.

"Excellent," Crusty said, stroking his W beard. He leaned close and whispered, "Because I need you to dig up my buried treasure."

Malcolm and Dandy turned to each other and grinned. Even with shackled hands, they gave each other a high five.

"Cool!" they shouted in unison.

The captain unlocked the cell. "I assume that means you're agreeable."

More than agreeable! Malcolm thought. *This is absolutely, totally awesome!*

Crusty unshackled them and led them topside. Squat looked over the captain's shoulder and winked.

Once they were on deck, the captain pulled out a spyglass and placed it to his eye. "See that small island down there?"

Malcolm leaned over and squinted. "Barely."

Crusty handed the spyglass to him and Malcolm gazed through the magnified lens. Even up close it was hard to see because of the clusters of palm trees.

"Down there is where my good-for-nothing brother buried my treasure," Crusty told them.

Dandy went to the rail and peeked over. "Why would he do a mean thing like that?"

"To hide it from me," Crusty said.

"Are you sure he buried it?" Dandy asked. "Maybe he kept it for himself."

"Not my brother. He was a mean, old bully. He just didn't want me to have it."

Malcolm lowered the spyglass and nodded. "I know how you feel. I have a sister who buried one of my video games once."

Crusty shook his head. "I don't know what a video game is, but that was very cruel of her."

"Even worse," Malcolm said, "she buried it in her underwear drawer."

The captain closed his eyes and shivered. "Siblings can be so unkind." He handed Malcolm the map and a shovel. "So, it is agreed. You will retrieve it?"

Malcolm looked down at the island, then back at Captain Scab. "Why didn't

you just dig it up yourself?"

"Because it's impossible!" he bellowed. "In case you've forgotten, this is a ghost ship. We can't make land. We're doomed to sail forever."

Oh yeah, Malcolm thought.

Squat did a jig and sang, "Forever. Forever. Forever and a day."

Nothing looks goofier than a dancing parrot with no legs.

"Uh, pardon me, Mr. Captain," Dandy said, tugging on Crusty's coat. "But if you can't make land, how are we supposed to get down there?"

Crusty put his fingers to his lips and whistled. Boggle-Eye scurried to him, holding a rope ladder.

Malcolm leaned over and gulped. "I hope it's a long ladder."

"It's long enough," Crusty said. He nodded and Boggle-Eye lowered the ladder.

"You won't be allowed back up till you have that treasure," Crusty told them. "Do you understand?"

Malcolm and Dandy shared a glance. "Yeah," Malcolm said. "We understand."

"And to make sure you don't try any tricky business, I'm sending Squat down with you."

The parrot leaped onto Dandy's head and squawked, "Land ho, mateys!"

Dandy crossed his eyes upward. "Ugh."

"Now go!" Crusty ordered as he gave them a shove.

Yo Ho Ho

Malcolm tucked the map into the waistband of his swim trunks. Gripping the shovel, he started down the wobbly ladder.

Dandy was above, making his way down too. Every few steps, Squat shouted, "Look out! Look out!"

Malcolm stopped and sighed. "Is there any way to shut that stupid bird up? He's driving me crazy."

"You've got it easy," Dandy said. "Every time he squawks, he claws into my head."

Malcolm started down again. "Maybe we can lock him inside the treasure chest."

"No! No! No!" Squat yelped.

Though it was a clunky trip down, they finally made it to the bottom of the ladder. But they were still a few feet from the ground.

Malcolm dropped the shovel. "Okay, here goes." He took a deep breath and hopped off, landing on the sand.

He brushed himself off, then looked up at Dandy. "Come on."

Dandy clutched the ladder tight. He stared down with a look of frozen horror on his face.

Malcolm shrugged. "It's not that far. Jump."

"It's not that," Dandy said. "I don't have my rain boots. My toes will be plump like red tomatoes."

Not this again! "Dandy, you have two choices. You can help me find the buried treasure, or you can spend the rest of your life locked up in that stinky cell."

"Or," Dandy added, "I can just hang here until you're done."

Squat rankled his feathers and yawped, "Let's go! Let's go!"

"Ow!" Dandy grabbed his head and—*Noooo!*—fell from the ladder. "You crazy pirate bird! That hurt."

Squat did a parrot dance on Dandy's noggin. "Yo ho ho. Yo ho ho."

Malcolm unrolled the map and pointed. "This *X* is where the treasure is buried." He placed his fingers on a drawing of a

long, curved tree. "It's twenty paces from this fallen palm."

Dandy leaned in close, examining it. "Are you sure it fell down? 'Cause it could've just grown sideways."

Malcolm rolled his eyes. "Trees don't grow sideways, Dandy."

"Maybe not where we're from," Dandy countered. "But this is a mysterious island. Trees might even grow upside down here."

Malcolm checked the map. "I don't see any upside-down trees drawn on."

"Of course not," Dandy said. "If they're upside down, then they're underneath the ground."

Malcolm huffed. "Fine. Let's look for a sideways palm."

Dandy glanced down at the sand seeping between his toes. "I don't guess you'll carry me piggyback again."

Malcolm picked up the shovel. "Maybe if you hop, you won't get beach blisters."

"Blisters! Blisters!" Squat echoed.

Dandy sagged like he'd just lost his favorite toy. "Okay. Let's go."

They hurried across the island, Malcolm jogging and Dandy hopping. They hadn't gone far when Squat shouted, "Uh-oh! Uh-oh!" He flapped and squawked and winged away.

"Where's he going?" Dandy asked. But just as he said it, a hard, fat coconut conked him on the head. "Ahhh! Why did those greedy pirates have to take my helmet?"

Another coconut fell, but this one bonked Malcolm on the head.

"What is going on?" He looked up. A couple of monkeys were squatted on top of a tree. "Hoo-hoo-hoo!" they chuckled. One plucked another coconut and fired.

"Stop that!" Malcolm shouted. *Wonk!* A direct hit. "Run, Dandy, run!"

The boys shot off, running as fast as they could. But there were more monkeys in other trees. Malcolm and Dandy darted and dodged like they were targets in a video game.

Suddenly, Malcolm screeched to a stop. Dandy smacked right into him and bounced back.

Malcolm pointed. "Look!" They were standing right in front of a palm tree that was growing sideways from the ground.

"I told you," Dandy gloated.

"But you didn't tell me about those."

There was a line of monkeys sitting on it, all holding coconuts. "Hoo-hoo-hoo!"

"How am I supposed to count off twenty paces if I keep getting whacked in the head?" he asked Dandy.

Dandy twitched his mouth, thinking. Then his eyes lit up. "I have an idea." He took the shovel from Malcolm. "Start counting."

Malcolm didn't know what Dandy had planned, but he didn't have time to ask. Captain Scab expected his treasure. And Malcolm's dad expected them to be ready at five. So Malcolm began pacing.

"One . . . two . . . three . . ."

"Hoo-hoo-hoo," the monkeys cheeped. They wound their arms and pitched one coconut at a time.

But Dandy was ready. He used the shovel like a baseball bat and hit every single one off into the ocean. Home run!

Luckily, the monkeys were amused. They bounced and sprang and clapped.

"Yeah, you can't pull one over on me," Dandy bragged.

Just then a coconut twonked him on the head. "What?" He looked up. "Squat!"

The no-legged parrot was dancing in the tree.

Thanks to Dandy, Malcolm found the right spot. "Bring the shovel," he called.

Dandy did. Malcolm took it and started digging.

"How deep do you think it's buried?" Dandy asked, standing back to avoid the flinging sand.

Malcolm didn't stop to look up. "Who knows."

He kept at it. He dug faster and faster and faster until . . . the shovel hit something hard. "I found it!"

Malcolm and Dandy both dropped to their knees and dug with their hands. They finally uncovered an old, withered case, crusted with sand.

Dandy grinned at Malcolm. "What do you think is in it?"

Malcolm grinned back. "What else? Crowns, gold statues, ancient coins."

They each grabbed a handle and tugged. After a few good heaves, they pulled it up and plopped it down next to the hole.

"Should we open it?" Dandy asked.

Malcolm wanted to open it more than anything in the world, but . . . He jiggled the old heart-shaped lock that was clamped to the hinges.

They both drooped.

Squat flew down and landed on Dandy's head. "No key. No key."

Dandy swatted at him. "Oh, hush!"

Malcolm got up and brushed the sand off his legs. "Oh well. Let's take it back."

Dandy stood too. "Maybe Captain Scab will be so grateful, he'll share some of this treasure with us."

"Or," Malcolm said, "maybe he'll just take it and lock us in that cell again."

Dandy grabbed one of the handles. "Ugh."

They trudged back, avoiding more mischievous monkeys with coconut bombs. The ladder still hung in the same spot.

Malcolm looked up, then down at the chest, then up again. They'd never be able to hop up that high. Especially with this bulky treasure chest.

"We may be stuck here forever," Dandy said.

"Nope. Nope." Squat flapped his wings and whistled.

A line of monkeys paraded up. "Hoo-hoo-hoo!" One of them hopped onto another monkey's shoulders. Then another climbed onto his. Pretty soon they'd made their own ladder up to the rope ladder. The bottom monkey grabbed the chest and passed it up one monkey at a time. "Hoo-hoo-hoo!"

Malcolm couldn't believe what he was seeing! "Genius!"

With the monkeys' help, Malcolm and Dandy made it up, too.

"Thanks!" Dandy said. "You're such nice monkeys." But just as he turned around, one of them bonked him on the back of the head with a coconut. "Ouch."

Walk the Plank

The captain must have known that Malcolm and Dandy couldn't lug that chest up by themselves. As soon as they were on the ladder, the crew of pirates heaved and hoed, pulling the boys up to the ship.

"Ahoy!" Crusty said as Squat flew onto his hat. "At last!" He rubbed his hands, greedily. Then he snapped his fingers at his crew. "Quick. Open it."

Scar-Cheek hurried over and kicked the rusty lock with this boot. It broke in two and clanged to the floor.

Malcolm and Dandy exchanged a look. It was that easy?

Crusty dropped to his knees. "My treasure!"

The boys moved in close. Dandy licked his lips. Malcolm's heart raced. He couldn't wait to see it.

The captain slowly opened the lid and carefully brought out . . . an accordion? "My squeezebox!" he shouted, seaweed dangling in his teeth. He hugged it to his chest. "I've missed you so, old friend."

"That's the treasure?" Malcolm asked.

"Yes," Crusty answered with tears in his eyes. "I couldn't bear spending eternity without it."

Then, with the worst squeaking and squawking ever, Captain Scab played his squeezebox. The ghostly pirates moaned and covered their ears.

Malcolm couldn't blame them. It was like nails on a chalkboard.

Crusty squeezed his squeezebox and sang, "I love being a pirate, sailing on the sea. And if somebody crosses me, I'll kick him in the knee."

"Uh, Mr. Captain?" Dandy said, tugging on Crusty's faded blue coat. "What happens to us?"

Crusty nodded to his crew. "They've done their job. Give them their belongings and let 'em go."

Yes! Malcolm wanted to sing, too. Finally they were going home. And he had a treasure far better than Crusty's. He

had all those great pictures. The first thing he'd do is call the Ghost Stalkers.

Captain Scab continued squeezing and singing as he strolled down below deck. Squat danced upon his hat.

"We're ready," Malcolm said. As soon as he was safe on land, he'd turn off his ghost detector and be rid of these pirates forever.

But the crew surrounded them, leering with hate-filled eyes.

Malcolm tapped his foot. "The captain said we could go," he reminded them.

"We heard 'im," Boggle-Eye sneered.

Dandy scootched closer to Malcolm. "You can't disobey orders."

"Oh, yes we can," the floppy hat pirate said. "It wasn't his brother who buried

that awful accordion. It was us. Now we have to listen to his terrible playing and singing forever."

Malcolm gulped.

"So, how will we punish them?" Scar-Cheek asked.

Boggle-Eye grinned. "Like we do with all scurvy dogs that board this ship. They'll walk the plank."

"No!" Malcolm begged. They were high up in a cloud. They'd never survive the fall.

Dandy raised his hand like he was at school. "I've got an idea. Why don't you sneak the squeezebox away from the captain while he's asleep? You can throw it overboard instead of us."

Boggle-Eye put a dagger to Dandy's chin. "'Cause the captain never sleeps."

"Oh." Dandy carefully pushed the point away with his finger.

"Get on the plank!" Boggle-Eye demanded.

Malcolm and Dandy glanced over. A large board had been placed on the edge of the ship.

"What do we do?" Dandy whispered.

Malcolm looked at the scruffy pirates, each holding a dagger or sword. "We walk the plank."

The boys inched back, slowly . . . slowly.

Scar-Cheek curled his lip. "Get on!"

Malcolm went first. Dandy stayed close, gripping the back of Malcolm's shirt. Once they got to the end, Malcolm finally looked down.

"It's not so bad, Dandy." They'd been passing through fog, not a cloud. He could see the pier below. But still, it was a long fall.

Scar-Cheek crept up behind them. "Don't forget this." He shoved Malcolm's pack at him.

"Wow, thanks," Malcolm said.

"Don't I get my armor?" Dandy asked.

Scar-Cheek narrowed his eyes. "I'll be needing those to protect me from that blasted parrot."

Malcolm could see how that would come in handy.

"Go!" Scar-Cheek booted Dandy. Dandy rammed into Malcolm, and they both went falling toward the sea.

The rough waters of the ocean churned under them. Malcolm clamped his eyes

shut, ready for impact. But instead of splashing down, he and Dandy plopped onto something soft and billowy.

They'd landed on the chute of a parasail. The parasailing ghost looked up at them and smiled. "Hitching a ride?" she asked.

Malcolm nodded. "Yes, ma'am."

She whisked them to shore, where they dropped down onto the sandy beach. Both boys fell back, out of breath.

"Thanks," Malcolm said to the ghost.

She winked. "Anytime." Then off she went, sailing down the coast.

"I can't believe we made it," Malcolm said. He quickly unzipped his pack and flipped off the ghost detector. Phew!

"I hope we never see the *Flying Hornswaggle* again," Dandy said.

Malcolm grinned. "We will." He pulled out his camera and . . . "No!"

"What's wrong?" Dandy asked.

Malcolm held it up. What was left of it. All the dials and buttons were busted. It looked like someone had stomped on it.

"I don't get it," Dandy said. "Why would Captain Scab break the camera, but not the ghost detector?"

Malcolm dropped the broken camera back in his pack. "Because as long as the ghost detector was on, we'd be able to find his treasure."

They both sat, staring out at the waves. What a day!

Then Dandy said, "Malcolm, I think we'd better go. My beach allergy is flaring up bad."

Malcolm pointed to Dandy's feet. "It's not a beach allergy, Dandy."

He was right. A dozen little fiddler crabs were pinching at Dandy's toes.

Dandy shot up and danced around. "Ow! Ow! Ow!"

Malcolm heard a horn honk. His dad pulled up. Just in time!

"Guess we won't be rich and famous," Dandy said as they trudged to the car.

"Sure we will," Malcolm told him. "Wait till the Ghost Stalkers see what we do next."

TOOLS OF THE TRADE: PIRATE SPEAK FOR THE GHOST HUNTER

From Ghost Detectors Malcolm and Dandy

Sometimes, ghost detectors need to know how to speak the languages of different ghosts! Here are five pirate phrases that came in handy for Malcolm and Dandy.

1. Ahoy - hello.

2. Clap 'em in irons - put them in handcuffs.

3. Landlubber - someone who lives on land, not a pirate.

4. Matey - friend.

5. Walk the plank - walk off the ship into the sea. If you walk the plank, you are left in the sea to drown or be eaten by sharks.